Timothy Dwight

Theodore Dwight Woolsey, D.D., LL.D.

Memorial address before the graduates of Yale University, June 24, 1890

Timothy Dwight

Theodore Dwight Woolsey, D.D., LL.D.
Memorial address before the graduates of Yale University, June 24, 1890

ISBN/EAN: 9783337036287

Printed in Europe, USA, Canada, Australia, Japan

Cover: Foto ©Raphael Reischuk / pixelio.de

More available books at **www.hansebooks.com**

Theodore Dwight Woolsey, D.D., LL.D.

MEMORIAL ADDRESS

BEFORE THE

GRADUATES OF YALE UNIVERSITY,

JUNE 24, 1890,

By PRESIDENT DWIGHT.

NEW HAVEN:

TUTTLE, MOREHOUSE & TAYLOR, PRINTERS.

1890.

PRESIDENT WOOLSEY.

MEMORIAL ADDRESS DELIVERED IN BATTELL CHAPEL,
JUNE 24TH, 1890, BY PRESIDENT DWIGHT.

DR. THEODORE DWIGHT WOOLSEY—what was his life in Yale College, and what was his work for it? Let me try to give you the simple story as best I may, and thus recall to your minds the thoughts and memories of other days. They will be inspiring memories and pleasant thoughts, I am sure, and will come to you most fittingly on this new anniversary of our University —the one which first follows the date of the ending of his long career.

I look backward in my thought, quite beyond the limits of my vision, to a fair autumn day in the year 1816, and I seem to see a slender, gentle youth coming forward with hesitation, and yet with confidence, to the doorway of entrance into the College life. His clear and penetrating eye bears witness of the intellect which illumines it, and his slightly bent figure suggests the scholarly habit and taste which soon make themselves manifest. Evidently of a cultured family and carrying in himself the inheritance of character and refinement, he wins the interest of all who test his fitness for the course of study which he desires to begin. Because of his name he is, of necessity, placed last in the list of the classmates who form the newly-entering company, but by reason of his power he gives promise at the outset of what is realized at the end. He is to be first among them all in the honors and successes belonging to the college years, and in the work and fame which pertain to the future. For the College itself and the students gathered within it for nearly half a century, he is to become a vitalizing, energizing force of intellectual and moral life. What an interesting day that autumn day was, when viewed as the opening of the coming time. It was the beginning of a life-course, whose record will ever remain as a cherished possession of this home of learning. The youth, who passed within the gates as its hours were closing, was in later years the man whom we revered as he walked along his scholarly and Christian way, beneath the elms, and ever turned our thoughts to the higher things.

We may trace the influences which rested upon him as he entered on his College life as far back as the earliest days of the College history. In the year 1709, his great-grandfather on the paternal side took his Bachelor's degree from the Collegiate school which had been founded only nine years before. Eleven years later, in 1720, his ancestor of the same generation on the maternal side, was sent forth as a young graduate to begin his illustrious career. It seems more than a fancy or a dream of the imagination that, from these two men, there came down, through the century that intervened, the power which made his life what it was, and was to be. The intellectual and spiritual force which dwelt in Jonathan Edwards, and constituted the grand inheritance that he gave to his children, may well have passed, in somewhat of its fullness, to this descendant of his family, as it had done to others in an earlier generation. And the inspiration of the genuine spirit of the College itself could scarcely have failed to come to him from one who had breathed it into himself at the very beginning, as had Benjamin Woolsey. The youth had surely a noble birth-right, and there was, as we might almost say, a Divine pointing, far away in the distance, toward the sphere and the character of his work, when the time for it should arrive. With these influences of the past, those which surrounded him as he began his course of study in the College must have coöperated most happily.

The men whom he met here were men of inspiring power, and men who, in the manliest and most generous way, had consecrated themselves to the institution. The chief among them was the great teacher of his generation—a man, according to the universal testimony of his contemporaries and pupils, of lofty character, of peculiar magnetic power, and of wonderful gifts of mind and heart. He was nearly allied by blood to the youthful student, and had been an object of his admiration in his earlier years. The life of this honored man came to its end, indeed, a few months after the date of which we are thinking, but we cannot doubt that the relationship and association between the two had given, before the end, much of the best impulse for true living to the one who was so ready to receive it. The other teachers were the men, then in the freshness and vigor of their manly years, who carried forward the institution so brilliantly and successfully during the first half of the present century—Day and Silliman and Kingsley. These men were full of the scholarly life and spirit which was then beginning to be awakened in the country. They were enthusiastically given up to the studies which they had chosen, and as enthusiastically devoted to the interests of the students and the College. They had taken into themselves the spirit of the founders of the institution. They were heirs of its freedom, its genuineness, its love of true learning, and its honest Christian faith. They believed in it, and lived for it. The lessons which such men taught were lessons characteristic of the place. They spoke not only of learning in itself, but of this home of learning, and carried always to the student's mind the influence of the latter intermingled with the more general influence of the former. The atmosphere of the College was thus adapted to the youth who was enrolling himself in its membership. It quickened, as he breathed it, the life-powers which had been given him from his ancestors. The Divine working for the early development of his educated life was in the line of the Divine pointing long before it began. The manhood, which was to be the result, could scarcely realize in itself any other character than that which had been prepared for it. The inheritance and the education united in making the intellectual scholar fashioned after the Yale type and characterized by the Yale spirit.

Such, as we picture him to ourselves, was Dr. Woolsey in the autumn of 1816—a bright, intelligent, studious youth, just closing his fifteenth year, with a mind eager for knowledge, a heart full of good impulses, a soul deep and rich enough to receive into itself whatever might strengthen it for right living. The gifts imparted by nature to himself and those which were transmitted to him from his ancestry combined to fit him for a life of highest usefulness in the intellectual sphere. They combined also, and in like measure, to make him ready, in his preparatory years, for everything pertaining to that sphere which could be offered to him. Once entered upon his College course, he gave himself readily and appreciatively to the appropriate work of the place. Immediately he took a prominent position as a scholar, commanding thereby the respect and esteem alike of his teachers and his fellow-students. He was retiring in his manner, unassuming in his disposition, indisposed to press himself forward. His intellectual clearness and vigor, however, were recognized by all. He grasped every subject, to which his thought was turned, with ease and with force. His mind was open on many sides. He was thoughtful, conscientious, earnest. He was sincere and truthful, having deep convictions, and being true to them with a manly honesty. He followed a quiet pathway through his college life, but it was a pathway of honor and success. He moved along his course in closest, yet friendly, rivalry with Solomon Stoddard, his classmate who afterwards stood in the foremost rank among the Latin scholars of his generation, and in kindly association with Leonard Bacon, who became one of the leaders of men for the fifty years that followed. He surpassed the former in his scholarly record in the college years, and won from the latter the word of commendation which pronounced him the first of the whole brotherhood of the class as a man of intellectual power.

On leaving College he gave himself, for a year, to the study of law under the instruction of the eminent jurist, Mr. Charles Chauncey, of Philadelphia, and then, for nearly two years, to the study of theology at Princeton. The former study he seems to have taken up for the purpose of mental discipline and the broadening of his education, but without any intention of entering upon the legal profession. The latter study was the one which he thought of as opening the way for him to the work of life. The Divinity School of Yale College was not established, as a separate part of the institution, when he went to Princeton, but after his return to New Haven as a Tutor in the College, in 1823, he was connected with the school for a year. He received license to preach near the end of his theological course, and we may believe that, for a time, he regarded himself as a candidate for the preacher's office. His self-distrust, however, with reference to his fitness to reach the high standard of this office, as he conceived of it, made him hesitate to undertake its duties. Moreover, the scholarly tastes, which had grown stronger with the passing of the few years since his graduation, were turning his mind and his desire towards another sphere of life. We may not doubt, also, that the keen-sighted mind of Professor Kingsley, under whose charge the linguistic studies in the College were then placed, perceived the capacity for true scholarship which the young graduate possessed, and that he used his strong influence to secure him for the scholar's field. The call to the Tutorship therefore came to him, no doubt, as a helpful thing in the determination of the question respecting his future career. While the position would afford him the opportunity of further prosecuting studies which were congenial to him, it would also give him a quiet resting-time for reflection and decision. To the College officers his acceptance of their invitation must have been most satisfactory, for it made it possible for them to test thoroughly his powers as a teacher, as they had already tested his capabilities as a student. In those days, the Tutors, to whom the instruction of the three younger classes was almost entirely intrusted, took charge, each of them, of all the studies of a particular division of a class. They were thus unable to concentrate their time and attention upon one branch of learning, as they may do now. It is easy to believe however, that, so far as was possible, the new Tutor turned his thought to linguistic studies. That he was of service to his pupils, by reason of his high ideal of scholarship, as well as his faithfulness as a teacher, is evident from the success of his subsequent career and from the testimony of the time. He continued in his office for two years, and then laid down its duties that he might engage in further study. Fortunately he was not limited in means, as many of his associates were. His father was a man of handsome property for that day, and was thus able to afford the son the privilege of a life in the foreign Universities—a privilege the enjoyment of which was much less frequent then, than it is at present. He pursued his Greek studies—the studies to which he particularly devoted himself —at Leipsic, Berlin and Bonn. In these places he came under the guidance and influence of the great Greek scholars of the period, Hermann, Bœckh, and Welcker. These learned and remarkable men were in the prime of life when he met them as a student—the oldest being fifty-six years old, and the others forty-three and forty-four. They were working under the

To The Graduates of Yale :

It is proposed to erect in the College Campus a bronze statue of the late President Woolsey, to be of heroic size. The design for the statue is by Professor John F. Weir, from studies made from life. It represents President Woolsey seated, holding a book, as if instructing a class. A photograph of the design accompanies this circular. The design has met with such approval from those who have seen it that a committee of graduates has been formed to procure the money necessary for the completion and erection of the statue. The estimated cost of the statue and of a suitable pedestal will be about $15,000.

To give the graduates of all departments, whether graduated under President Woolsey or not, an opportunity to share in this memorial to one whose long and notable services to the University and whose personal character and scholarly achievements made him one of the most eminent men of his time, the committee have thought best to make a general appeal for the money they have been asked to raise.

If each of the living graduates of Yale will contribute Ten Dollars the completion of the fund will be assured. It is hoped that nearly all will be able and willing to promptly aid the object to that extent.

If as the Committee hope their should be any surplus it will be turned over to the Woolsey Fund.

Contributions may be sent to M. Dwight Collier, Esq., 45 Pine Street, New York, Secretary of the Committee. Cheques should be made payable to order of Brayton Ives, Esq., treasurer.

Dated New York, June 9, 1890.

General Committee.

TIMOTHY DWIGHT,
President Yale University, Chairman.

Prof. HUBERT A. NEWTON,
Yale College.

Prof. HENRY W. FARNAM,
Yale College.

Prof. WILLIAM K. TOWNSEND,
Yale Law School.

Prof. FRANCIS WAYLAND,
Yale Law School.

Prof. GEORGE J. BRUSH,
Sheffield Scientific School.

Dr. WM. H. CARMALT,
Yale Medical School.

Prof. GEORGE P. FISHER,
Yale Theological School.

BRAYTON IVES (Treasurer),
New York City.

Hon. CHAUNCEY M. DEPEW,
New York City.

EDWARD W. LAMBERT, M.D.,
New York City.

Rev. RODERICK TERRY,
New York City.

WILLIAM P. DIXON,
New York City.

FREDERIC H. BETTS,
New York City.

HOWARD MANSFIELD,
New York City.

WILLIAM C. GULLIVER,
New York City.

FREDERIC W. VANDERBILT,
New York City.

Hon. WILLIAM M. EVARTS,
New York City.

Hon. EDWARDS PIERREPONT,
New York City.

GEORGE DE F. LORD,
New York City.

BUCHANAN WINTHROP,
New York City.

Hon. WILLIAM C. WHITNEY,
New York City.

M. C. D. BORDEN,
New York City.

THOMAS C. SLOANE,
New York City.

ARTHUR M. DODGE,
New York City.

M. DWIGHT COLLIER, Secretary,
New York City.

I. FREDERIC KERNOCHAN,
New York City.

Hon. JAMES M. VARNUM,
New York City.

BENJAMIN D. SILLIMAN,
Brooklyn, N. Y.

FREDERIC A. WARD,
Brooklyn, N. Y.

JAMES L. WHITNEY,
Boston, Mass.

J. MONTGOMERY SEARS,
Boston, Mass.

Prest. ANDREW D. WHITE,
Ithaca, N. Y.

SAMUEL C. PERKINS,
Philadelphia, Pa.

SAMUEL H. HOLLINGSWORTH,
Philadelphia, Pa.

WILSON S. BISSELL,
Buffalo, N. Y.

Hon. RANDALL L. GIBSON,
Washington, D. C.

ARNOLD HAGUE,
Washington, D. C.

Hon. THOMAS L. BAYNE,
New Orleans, La.

Rev. JOSEPH H. TWICHELL,
Hartford, Conn.

Hon. WILLIAM TAFT,
Cincinnati, Ohio.

THORNTON M. HINKLE,
Cincinnati, Ohio.

FRED. N. JUDSON,
St. Louis, Mo.

JAMES M. ALLEN,
San Francisco, Cal.

JAMES COFFIN,
San Francisco, Cal.

CHARLES W. BINGHAM,
Cleveland, Ohio.

WILLIAM R. BELKNAP,
Louisville, Ky

EDWARD G. MASON,
Chicago, Ill.

JAMES S. NORTON,
Chicago, Ill.

STANFORD NEWELL,
St. Paul, Minn.

GEORGE P. WETMORE,
Newport, R. I.

Executive Committee.

FREDERIC H. BETTS, Chairman.

BRAYTON IVES, Treasurer

M. DWIGHT COLLIER, Secretary.

TIMOTHY DWIGHT, D.D. (Ex-officio member),
E. W. LAMBERT,
WM. P. DIXON.

HOWARD MANSFIELD,
I. FREDERIC KERNOCHAN.

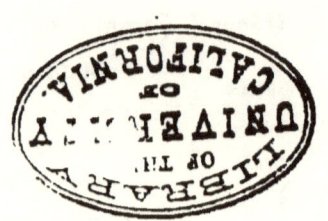

impulse and inspiration of their growing fame. To sit in their lecture rooms and listen to their words was, for such a young man, a privilege indeed. With all the facilities which we now enjoy, and with the results of German learning so largely in our hands, we can scarcely realize what an impulse must have been given him, as he breathed the atmosphere of those Universities and received the instruction of their Professors. It was a *new world* for the *inner life* which he found himself continually entering, as he was passing three happy years in the *old world* of which he had often thought in the former days. It was a world in which he was always receiving new knowledge, new life-power as a scholar, and new thoughts which would become seed-thoughts for all the future. The best influence of a student's life abroad is this stimulating and quickening influence. But, in that day, this influence added its gift to a measure of learning which was inaccessible at home, and a twofold blessing was thus bestowed upon the receptive mind. We cannot doubt that the blessing came in both of its forms to the earnest young graduate and tutor from Yale.

When the three years of foreign residence and travel had come to their end, he turned his face homeward. These years, with all which they had given him in the matter of inspiration and of learning, had borne him forward towards the hour of inevitable decision as to his life's career. The self-distrust with reference to his fitness for the ministry of the gospel had not diminished. At the same time, his love for the scholar's work and his desire to devote himself to it had naturally, and as if of necessity, increased. He returned to America, therefore, with doubtful mind. The opportunities might not open in the direction in which his wishes were moving. He must wait for the light which a day still in the future might throw upon his pathway. The Divine call would come, no doubt, in its own time, but it was not as yet possible to hear it. His experience was like that of many a young scholar, since that day, who has left the student-years abroad with mingled joy and sorrow—joy in the brightness and certainty of the season just closing for him, and sorrow for the uncertainty and possible disappointment of the season just opening. For more than one of us here present to-day, the voyage homeward from the old world has been attended, as we may well remember, with the same questioning as to the summons of duty and the possibilities of the future. But the uncertainties must have been much greater sixty years ago than they are now, for that was a time of small things in the field of University education. Places were few, endowments were very limited, the public demands were in their beginnings rather than their fullness. College teaching was scarcely, as yet, in any such sense a profession that a young man could, without presumption, choose it for himself, after the manner in which he might choose one of the other professions. We are living to-day in a far happier period, in this regard, than that in which the determination of this youthful scholar's course had to be made.

The plan of God for his life, however, was developing itself, though its clear revelation was delayed a little. The labors, and even the questionings, of the years had not been without a purpose. The mind and character were fitted by them for the sphere which would be divinely opened, and in which all the preparation would work into large and rich results.

When he reached his home on his return from Europe, he was twenty-eight or twenty-nine years of age. He seems not to have waited long before he received some signs of recognition as a scholar of promise. One or two offers were made to him of professorships, or permanent positions in different institutions of learning. But none of these offers seemed to him to bear in themselves the call of duty, and he declined them. I well remember the words which he said to me, thirty years afterwards, concerning one of these positions, when, on a certain day in 1858. I went to his room to consult with him respecting the offer of a place, which I had myself just then been asked to consider. " When I was young, as you are," he said, " I was called to a professorship in a distant state, and I was almost ready to accept it. But, by the blessing of God, I did not accept it; and a little while afterwards I was called to New Haven, and my life has been spent here. Wait a little, as I did, if you *can* wait, is my advice to you."—And by the blessing of God, I followed his advice.

The little time passed by, and the way was opened for him to come to Yale College. He entered on the professorship of the Greek Language and Literature in the autumn of 1831, when he was just at the end of his thirtieth year. The faculty of the Academical Department of the College consisted at that time of five professors, besides himself, seven tutors, and the President. President Day and Professors Silliman and Kingsley had been in the service of the College, as permanent officers, since 1803 to 1805. They were, accordingly, in the faculty of instruction when he entered college, and had been in their work for more than ten years before that time. Professors Fitch and Goodrich had received their appointment after the death of Dr. Dwight, and at the beginning of Mr. Woolsey's Sophomore year. Professor Olmsted had entered upon his duties in 1825. The reception into their company and fellowship of such an intelligent and gifted student, and the establishment of a new chair for his occupancy, must have been a matter of deepest satisfaction to all these older professors. The foundation of a new chair was a rare thing in those days. The discovery of such a man is a rare thing in any age. There were three hundred and thirty-one students in this department of the College at the opening of that year. The relation of this number of students to the number of permanent officers, which has just been mentioned, is suggestive for the men of to-day, and especially when we think of the work of education, which was done here for years through the efforts of these self-denying teachers.

Immediately upon the entrance of Professor Woolsey on the duties of his office, the work of the Greek department, of which Professor Kingsley had previously had charge in connection with the Latin department, was passed into his hands. He brought with him to the work the accuracy and breadth of scholarship, which had been acquired or developed in Germany, and the inspiration of mind which had there been given him. Not far from the age of the students, comparatively speaking, and with the freshness of new ideas and, in some degree, of new methods, he naturally stirred the minds of his pupils to a deeper and more permanent interest in the studies to which he called them. They saw in him the true scholar, who had gained much for himself from the most beautiful of all languages, and they were impelled by the manifestation of his scholarly life, as well as by his daily instructions. My own personal recollections do not go back to that time. But I remember what I heard as a young boy, ten or twelve years later, from those who were older than myself, and I am assured that much of new life came into the whole College community by reason of the presence of the young professor. His thoughts moved in many directions; his reading was extensive; his intellectual interests were wide-reaching; and his aspirations in the sphere of learning and truth were high and manly. He was, therefore, always ready to coöperate with others like himself in all that would elevate, in a literary and scholarly way, the daily life of the College community, and the social life of the educated circle of the city in which he moved.

Very soon after he began his work of instruction as a professor, he undertook the preparation of text books for his students. The editions of the Greek classics which were then at command in this country were very imperfect. Nothing of value, or very little, had yet been published as the result of American scholarship. The riches of German learning and German methods had not been placed in our possession. Perceiving the need, he set himself to the work of supplying it. With the inspiration of his fine taste and his sense of beauty in thought and in poetry, he directed his studies to the tragedies of the great Greek poets, and brought them before the minds of his pupils. His editions of different plays of Aeschylus, Sophocles, and Euripides appeared as early as 1834, 1835, and 1837. They introduced a new era in Greek scholarship for our Colleges, and were so abundant in learning and so fully in accordance with the true method, that they long retained their complete hold upon teachers everywhere. Even now, after the great progress which has been made during the past thirty years, these works have the recognition of all scholars, who look into them, as worthy of the highest esteem. A few years later than 1837, he turned his thought to the work of editing Plato's Dialogues, and in 1843 the edition .of the Gorgias was published. This volume was characterized by the same excellences as those which had marked the volumes containing the tragedies. His intention, it is believed, was to prepare a series of such volumes for the illustration of Plato's thoughts. But this proved to be the only one, to the publication of which he was able to give his efforts. By reason of the new office which he was called three years afterwards to assume, his sphere of teaching was changed, and his scholarly efforts were demanded in other and far different lines. He laid aside his Greek instruction and his special work as a Greek scholar with reluctance. The summons of duty, however, was too clear to be refused. He was to become a greater and more useful man elsewhere.

The period of Mr. Woolsey's professorship extended from 1831 to 1846. During this period he was, beyond question, the rising scholar of the College—the one to whom the younger men looked with peculiar hope for the future, and the one in whom the older men trusted for the continuance to another generation of that spirit of sound learning which had dwelt in themselves. In the review of his professorial life we must take hold upon the recollections of men who are, at the present date, from sixty-five to eighty years of age. To most of the graduates now living it is a review of a historical period, almost half a century having elapsed since it came to its close. But it is not too much to say, that of the men to whom I have alluded, and whose time of College study was in that period, there are none who do not recall with pleasure the Greek instructor of their youth. They saw in him an honest student; a man of true culture; a teacher who demanded much of them, indeed, but was, at the same time, ready to open much before their vision; a friend who would ever inspire them with his own love of knowledge, and show them by his own example, how much better it was to be, than only to seem to be. As a disciplinarian he was strict, but yet always just. He was quick in temper, in decision, and in action, and was ready to sustain the authority of the College government at all times. But he was never disposed to play, as some men are, with suspicions or half suspicions, and thus try to involve a supposed offender—by assuming to know more than was really known—in a confession of what he had done, or perchance of what he had not done. He was a manly man here, as everywhere. Though sometimes stern, he was acknowledged by all to be even-handed and fair-minded. He was thus respected, even by those with whom he felt compelled to deal severely. They were persuaded that he intended to do precisely what was right; and they honored the man, though they might suffer from his act.

The discipline of the College community was a different matter in those days from what it is now, and a matter which involved many more difficulties. The system adopted and carried out was largely the same with that which had been in existence a hundred years before. It was founded on the idea that a College government must be displaying its authority all the time. It took little account of the differences between young men and old men. It was suspicious of wrong everywhere, and had no thought of removing wrong except by violent measures. It lost sight of human nature, and attempted to regulate everything by a theory. We may not wonder that its successes were not uninterrupted, and that when they were realized, it was often after a hard struggle in which evil passion had been largely aroused. It was an unpropitious day for a young professor to attempt to introduce new ideas. It was a day in which he could scarcely be expected to have such ideas. The most that he could do was to carry on the system, so far as he was himself concerned, in a just and honorable way. This Mr. Woolsey did ; and he did it fearlessly, as he did everything. It ought to be said also, that the student community was itself—independently of the government and its measures or theories—of a less orderly character than it is to-day. The progress of half a century and more has done much to humanize the subjects of College authority, as well as much to soften and make more reasonable the administration of it. The rebellions of sixty years ago and the disorders of ten and twenty years later were not due simply to the methods of governing. They were due also, and in no inconsiderable measure, to the half-civilized condition—if we may use this strong expression to describe it, for the sake of emphasis—in which the students themselves were when they came into the College community. Happily those days have passed away— as we may trust, forever. It is a rare thing in this better age,

when some unworthy alien to the true University spirit breaks
in upon the quiet and orderly life of the home of learning with
some act of violent disturbance or vandalism, such as was often
repeated, in all our institutions, in the earlier days. And if such
an act ever occurs now, it violates the spirit of the students, as
truly it does that of other educated gentlemen.

The change in the system of government had its earliest
beginnings some years after the close of Mr. Woolsey's term
as professor, and at a time which is remembered as coincident
with the official life of two or three of the oldest officers now
in active service. The beginning was the work of one or two
of the young men holding tutorships in the College, who had
breathed a new spirit and were believers in a new era. They
believed in other young men a little younger than themselves,
and in governing them by persuasion, and friendship, and sweet
reasonableness ; and as they believed, they tried the new
system, with the happiest results for themselves and the most
hopeful promise for the future. There are letters of Dr.
Woolsey which I have seen since his death, and other letters
also addressed to him, which show who led in this movement
for the better time. The reward of the movement is enjoyed
by the faculty and students alike to-day. The teachers and
their pupils are friends in the kindliest friendship now, and
the sons of the University, whether younger or older, are what
they ought to be—a true brotherhood. It was an honor to Dr.
Woolsey's administration that the change began in its earlier
years, and that he had the open mind to appreciate the possibilities of good which it might involve in itself.

His administration had its beginning in the autumn of 1846.
He was at that time just forty-five years of age—one year
older than President Day was when he entered upon the
Presidential office, and two years older than the first President
Dwight, when he was called to the same duties. He was thus

at the opening of the most mature and vigorous portion of his life. He was in sympathy with the thoughts and wants of the new generation, while he was old enough to enter into the feelings of his older colleagues, and to keep firmly what they committed to him. He was an intelligent, cultured scholar, just ready for the dawning scholarly age. It was said, twenty years ago, by a prominent graduate of our College, when comparing this institution with another which he mentioned, that *men* had made the Presidents of that institution, but *God* had made the Presidents of Yale. No wonder that he made this statement respecting Yale College, as he was thinking of President Woolsey, whose term of office was not then ended, and of his two predecessors. For the great creative period of the College history, when new and comprehensive plans for the long future were to be laid, and far-reaching thoughts of what the institution ought to be, and might become, were to be originated, no man could have been more wonderfully fitted by qualities both of mind and soul, than was the first President Dwight. For the generation which followed, in which the results of the former work were to be gathered, and the foundations already laid were to be made secure,—when traditions were to be established, and the quiet order of successful movement was to be realized, President Day was the man of all men. Calm, peaceful, wise with the wisdom of conservatism, venerable in character at the beginning, and in years also at the end,—his dignified bearing a reminder of order and stability, and his very presence a benediction,—who could have appeared to preside over the quieter age so fitly as he ?

The time had arrived, at the close of Dr. Day's administration, when a new forward movement was needed. Everything was ready for the development of sound learning, and of true scholarship in every line, in a far greater degree than had been known, or had even been possible, at any earlier period. A

man adapted to the time was needed. For such a man a grand
opportunity was presenting itself. It is not strange, therefore,
that when, to the regret of all, Dr. Day felt obliged by reason
of his far advanced age to resign his office, the minds of those
who were interested in the welfare of the College were at once
turned to Professor Woolsey as the one to succeed him. Mr.
Woolsey had been absent from home, and residing or traveling
in Europe, for several months previous to this time, and was
intending to remain abroad until the opening of the next College year. Without his knowledge, therefore, and apparently
without any thought on his part as to what was taking place,
public opinion in the institution was settling itself in the con-
viction that he ought to be made the new President. His
friend Professor Kingsley, who had watched his career from
the beginning with deep interest, communicated to him the
sentiment in his favor a short time before his return to
America. Mr. Woolsey appears to have been genuinely sur-
prised at the choice which his friends and associates seemed, in
their own thoughts, to be determining. He had no desire for
the position, and did not regard himself as specially fitted for
it. By reason of the extraordinarily high esteem which, in
common with all his colleagues, he had for President Day, he
doubtless felt a peculiar distrust of himself as the thought of
entering into the office which had been so honorably filled was
presented to him. How could he take the place and carry forward the work of so wise, so able, so serene, so holy a man—
the holiest and most blameless, as he afterwards said when
speaking of him, of all the men whom he had ever known.
His reply to Professor Kingsley was an unfavorable one ; and
subsequently when the Corporation elected him to the Presidency and formally offered it to his acceptance, he gave a nega-
tive answer to their request.

In the light of the following time, such a feeling of hesitation and inadequacy seems strange to the reader of the history.

That one who accomplished so great a work, and whose success was assured from the very beginning of his administration, should have deemed himself unequal to the requirements of the place, may well appear remarkable. That one whose Christian character was a power for good in hundreds of lives for a quarter of a century, and whose prayers and preaching impressed every hearer with a sense of the reality and richness of the soul's life beneath and behind them, should have doubted his fitness for ordination to the Christian ministry, will seem even more remarkable. But so it was. These scruples and questionings as to himself and his qualifications had to be overcome by the earnest persuasion of his friends, before he would consent to withdraw his refusal of the offer of the Corporation and accept the new position. With reluctance, however, and at a late moment, he yielded ; and every one, except himself, had an unmingled satisfaction. This satisfaction grew deeper and more satisfying as the twenty-five years of his Presidency moved forward. He was the man for the era, even as those who had preceded him had been the men for their times. He was summoned of God, as all believed, to a work the importance and blessing of which for our College cannot be over-estimated.

He was inaugurated as President on the 21st of October, 1846. On the same day, he received ordination as a minister of the gospel, and thus realized the full significance of his early thought and study in preparation for the preacher's work. That the setting apart of the new President to the ministerial office was the initial step in the entrance-way to the Presidential duties was, in Dr. Woolsey's case, a ground for thankfulness on the part of every friend of Yale College and every student within its walls. The life of Dr. Woolsey would have lost a large part—the richest and most useful part—of its fruit-bearing power in other lives, had he not lived among his

pupils as a Christian minister. The character of many noble men, who studied here during the years of his administration, bears witness to-day of what he did for them by reason of his testimony, as a preacher, to the truth of God. The atmos- phere of the College was purer, and the standard of its living higher, because he told here so often the Christian story. His administrative work, his instruction, and his preaching moved to a common end—the end of right thinking and pure living on the part of all who came under his influence.

The four main thoughts of Dr. Woolsey's inaugural address suggest to us the great ideas under the influence of which he carried forward his work. He spoke on the subject of the Christian teacher and the character of his teaching. It is impressive to our minds, as we think of the man to-day, to recall what he said at the beginning of his new service in the College. The Christian instructor, he said, will value training more than knowledge; he will study to improve all parts of the mind; he will estimate education, not so much by its relation to immediate ends of a practical sort, as by its relation to higher ends, far more important than success in a profession and the power of acquiring wealth and honor; and he will, as far as lies within the range of his department, lead the minds of his pupils up to God. How characteristic these thoughts were of the man. How suggestive they were of that develop- ment of scholarship and learning under the power and guiding influence of the Christian faith, which he was to be instru- mental in securing on these grounds during the quarter of a century that followed. How strikingly they lead us backward to the early days when Jonathan Edwards· and Benjamin Woolsey breathed the College atmosphere, and when the founders of the institution consecrated it to the work of diffus- ing light and truth, as they asked, first of all, the benediction of the Divine Father.

Previous to the beginning of Dr. Woolsey's official term, the President had had under his charge the instruction of the Senior Class in Mental and Moral Philosophy. In the year 1846, however, a Professorship in this department of study was established. A new arrangement of duties, accordingly, became necessary, and the incoming President turned aside to other studies. He devoted himself to the department of History, for the instruction in which he had conspicuous qualifications and a strongly-developed taste. He added to his work in History the teaching of Political Economy during the later portion of the Senior year. In connection with this arrangement, a much more full preparation of the students in these important branches was secured, than had been possible before. Dr. Woolsey's knowledge of history was abundant and accurate. He had a remarkable tenacity of memory, which enabled him to hold in his mind a great mass of facts and events. He had also the philosophical faculty, which fitted him to adjust the relations of things, and which made History for him not merely a collection of facts, but a science. This latter faculty was so dominant in his mind that, though himself possessed of such unusual power of recollecting all that he had learned, he was impatient of *memoriter* recitations on the part of his students, and thought little of the youth who could not rise above them. He desired his pupils to reason about what they knew ; and tried, according to his ability and opportunity, to make them thinking men. For nearly twenty years he continued his instruction of the classes in History. The foundation for a chair in this branch of study, however, having been secured in 1865, he willingly passed this portion of his teaching to another and younger man, and gave himself to the more full development of the other section of his work. From this time forward he accomplished more and more in Political Science and International Law—studies in which he had already, before

this, rendered important service. He became, as we all know, a distinguished authority in International Law—recognized for his ability and learning in Europe, as well as throughout America. The first edition of his work on this subject was published as early as 1860, but it was enlarged and improved afterward, and passed through five editions in this country, and two in England—the last having appeared in 1879 in New York and London. His large work on Political Science was published several years after the close of his Presidential term, in 1877, and was an evidence of the activity of his mind, and of his earnestness in work, even when he had already become an old man. His power as a teacher was more conspicuous in these departments than it had been in history. His influence was a constantly growing one, and the young men in the successive Senior Classes met him with an ever-increasing admiration. Had he possessed the rare gift of magnetism as a teacher —a gift which he was himself conscious of not possessing, as he once frankly stated to me, and a gift which, so far as my knowledge of teachers extends, is far more rare than any other —he would have realized a completeness in his work for his students, in some aspects of it, which was not fully attained. But he had other and perhaps greater gifts in an extraordinary measure, and by means of them he left an impression on the students' minds which could never be forgotten. He had not the peculiar personal gift of inspiration for others which so strikingly characterized the late Dr. Mark Hopkins, but he lived as truly in the inmost lives of his pupils, though after a somewhat different manner, as did that eminent College teacher. To his instruction and the inspiring power of· his scholarship, as I met him in the earliest years of my life as a graduate, I owe my own best impulses as a student, and I cannot doubt that the experience of many others bears the same testimony which mine bears. He was, of all the men whom I have ever seen, the one who most fully realized my ideal of a scholar.

It is remarkable how widely his scholarly power reached. He turned his course from that of a Greek professor, whose studies and attainments had placed him in the foremost rank, to that of a teacher of History and Political Science, and then to that of a lecturer and writer on International Law; and in each science, in its order, he was as successful and able as he had been in the field which he first entered. Moreover, when he had finished his whole work in the College, he returned to that first field, once more, as he was called to a membership in the Committee for the Revision of the English Version of the New Testament. In that body of leading scholars in their own department, he was, all things considered, the leading man. His scholarship, for breadth and richness and accuracy, when measured together and in their mutual relations, was unequaled by that of any other person in the Company. His theological learning was also abundant, and as a preacher of intellectual force, of suggestive thought, of insight into the human soul, and of clear apprehension of the gospel truth, he was among the ablest in the country. He was, moreover, a keen observer of public life, an independent thinker in politics, an educated citizen of the highest type, and fully qualified to discuss the most important questions with men who had given all their thoughts and studies to the consideration of them. The fact that such a man was in the College community and that each Senior Class could meet him daily in the lecture-room was, indeed, an inspiration for all. Every graduate, as he left the institution, was conscious that he had been in contact with a truly great man.

In the administrative work of the College pertaining to the Presidential office, Dr. Woolsey was successful. The governmental element was strong in his character. He was born to command. But as he grew older, and as the changes of time came, he was able to appreciate the weaknesses of the old system of government to which allusion has already been made. He could understand the authority of love, as well as that of force, and was far from thinking that because a thing had come down from the past, it must necessarily be firmly held as an undoubted good. At the very beginning of his official term, he relaxed the rule of early morning prayers, so far that they were placed half an hour later than they had been, in the time of his predecessor. Ten years afterwards, he consented to the entire abolishing of the old arrangement, and established the present system, in accordance with which we meet together for our daily worship at eight o'clock. In his intercourse with students under discipline also, he dealt with them in a manly way, as has been said a few moments since, and, though strict and firm in his application of the law, he respected the manhood in every man whom he met. The true proportion of the paternal and governmental elements in administration is never realized in this world. Men are ever excessive on the one side or the other, and the result is ever more or less of weakness. That Dr. Woolsey had more of the governmental element in his work as an administrative officer of the College, than was in accordance with the ideal measure, cannot be questioned. So had all the College officers of his generation, and he was in a peculiar degree a man of imperious nature. But he had much of tenderness in the depths of his soul, and he did not have a closed mind.

So far as discipline was related to studies, Dr. Woolsey made a marked advance upon the preceding time. He was enabled to do this partly by the additions to the force of instructors which the increase of endowments rendered possible. But it was partly the result of his high ideal of scholarship and his views respecting the demands for more thorough education. The Senior year was made much more effective and useful than ever before. Examinations of a far higher order were introduced, and the spirit of study throughout the entire College was called forth. Every student felt that a new life was infused into the institution. Every one knew that the original source of that life was the President. His inspiration, his courage, and his example moved the whole community. He did a great work, in this way, not only for this College, but for all Colleges throughout the country. He was a light and a power in the opening era of true scholarship.

To be such a light and power, and to do such a work for this institution, was his mission, to which he was called of God. The three successive eras had discovered their own men. It was a divine blessing to Yale College, that they were raised up to meet its needs, and that they appeared in the true order. That no one of them did the work of another, was no lessening of their greatness. They moved forward to the limit of their time, and left the future, and its planning and working, for those who should follow them. That future, whatever may be accomplished within it, will rest in no small measure upon what they did in their day.

The passing of a quarter of a century from the date of his entering, at the age of forty-five, upon the Presidency reminded Dr. Woolsey that he was reaching the limit of seventy years. He had long since determined to offer his resignation when he should arrive at this age, and no change of purpose came at the end. He laid aside his office when he was yet in the full vigor of his mental power, and when his associates in instruction and government would have willingly seen him still longer continuing his duties. He was himself persuaded, however, of the wisdom of his decision. He was assured in his own mind that the fitting time for him to retire had come. I recall an interview which, by accident, I myself had with him just at that season, in the course of which he said—in response to my suggestion that his resignation would be a loss to the College:

No : the hour has arrived for others to carry forward the work. His wisdom was greater than that of those who wished him to remain in his office. He retired to a rich, honorable, grand life of old age—with confidence in those whom he left behind him in the institution which he loved, and in the consciousness of the reverential regard of all.

The years from 1871 to 1881—from the close of his own seventieth year to the close of his eightieth—were filled with scholarly work. He devoted his time largely to preparing or revising his books which were issued during this period, and to the studies in the New Testament Greek which were connected with the work of Bible Revision. It was most pleasant to see how interested he was in this quiet work. His mind moved towards the new things as happily as it had moved, in other days, towards the old things. The evening time was bright with its own peculiar light. The kindly affection and esteem of all men, far and wide through the land, gathered about him more largely than ever before, and he enjoyed the manifestation of the feeling with a deep and tender satisfaction. With all his force and energy and self-reliance, he had a sort of childlike dependence on others, which it was most interesting to witness in such a man. When the days of administration and teaching and public duty were ended, he seemed to enter into an appreciative sense of the loving relation between himself and other men, which was new in its fullness and its blessing.

His connection with the College was not wholly severed during these years, for at the termination of his Presidency he was elected a member of the Corporation. His advice and the results of his experience were thus easily made available, whenever there was need. The frequent consideration of important questions, also, kept alive his interest in the present life of the College. He rendered the institution the service which he could give as a friend who had long known its history and its wants, and quickened his love for it by means of every service. Even until he had nearly reached the age of eighty-four he retained this office, leaving it only a single year before the close of the Presidency of his successor. The relations between him and President Porter were ever most intimate and confidential. It will always be a pleasant remembrance to me, that his last official act, if we may call it such, was in connection with my own entrance upon the Presidential office. His presence at the services of the inauguration seemed to unite the present with the past, and to make the line of historic development in the institution a continuous, unbroken line.

The three years that followed brought for him with themselves greater infirmities of far advanced life, and the work of his long career of necessity ceased. The passing to the other life, he said to a friend, was that to which he looked forward as the next great event which now awaited him. The days and months moved onward through these years, and on the morning of the first day of July, 1889, the end came. We laid his body tenderly and lovingly in its last resting place, four days afterwards, on a beautiful summer afternoon. Our thoughts followed him within the veil, and we rejoiced in hope of the future.

Such is the story, briefly told in an hour—to be filled out into completeness, and perfected as with a living reality, by the grateful memories of all who have listened to it. The man, of whom it has given its picture, was a man of clear and vigorous and powerful mind, of tender and loving, yet strong heart, of rich, deep, earnest soul. He was a scholar unsurpassed in his generation; a teacher who impressed all his pupils, and moved to earnestness in study and life the best among them; a preacher whose thoughts were ever fresh and stimulating, and whose insight into the workings of human character was so penetrating that his words had for every hearer the emphasis of the truth. He was honest, sincere, faithful, just—a manly man; a believing Christian; a disciple of the Lord Jesus, who laid hold upon the kingdom of God and endured as seeing the invisible.

That Dr. Woolsey was a faultless man, I would not say. He would not himself have said it, nor have wished it said concerning him. He had faults which, strangely enough, have been praised as striking virtues by friendly critics since his death, and which were imitated by some of his admirers before his death far more than his virtues were. But the faults were intermingled with the greatness of the man, and they did not destroy the greatness. · They belonged to his native character, partly, and partly to the age in which he was educated. He fought them manfully wherever he recognized them, and grew, as all noblest Christian men do, into the good, and out of the attendant evil, more and more as life passed on to its later stages. He was indeed a noble Christian man, whose life was a testimony to manliness and truth, and an inspiration to duty for us all. My office is not to be his biographer—would that some truly appreciative friend might render this loving service. It is not to dissect, and describe in every part, his character. The historian, at some future day, may do this, when the pupils and the friends who revered him have passed on in their journey. We knew him, and we thank God that we did. We believe in the true, sincere, deep life of the human soul more fully and undoubtingly because we knew him, and we thank God for the blessing of the belief.

Rather would I turn aside from all that the biographer might think of or describe, and bring these commemorative words to their ending with the remembrance of what he did for myself; of the impulse which he gave me in my studies long years ago when, with two or three young graduates, I

met him in the freedom of his own room, and read Thucydides
and Pindar under his instruction; and of the generous expression of his approval of my course in the Tutorial office, where I
thought I saw a light sometimes and followed it, which he did
not see; and of the kindly advice he gave me with reference
to my life-work when I was questioning, in a German University, what that work should be; and of the equal kindness
of his judgment, as he asked me to remain at Yale in a professorship; and of the confidence which he ever afterwards
manifested in me and my associates, as we were building up
one of the schools of learning here; and of the hearty wel-
come which he gave me as I entered into the succession of the
Presidents of the institution. He was a generous friend
through all the course, whose life was vitally related to my
own at different stages, and whose thoughts never changed
from the beginning. From out of the enjoyment and rich
experience of my own life in Yale College, I look forth upon
his life, and I feel that it may well be a sacred memory.
And then, as I look upon one and another of the educated men
who are now before me, and think of the College where they
were taught and the University into which it has grown, I find
the answer coming from within myself, and from within their
minds and hearts also, to the question: What was the life in
this home of learning—our early home—and what was the
work on its behalf, which are represented to our thought and
memory by the name of Theodore Dwight Woolsey.